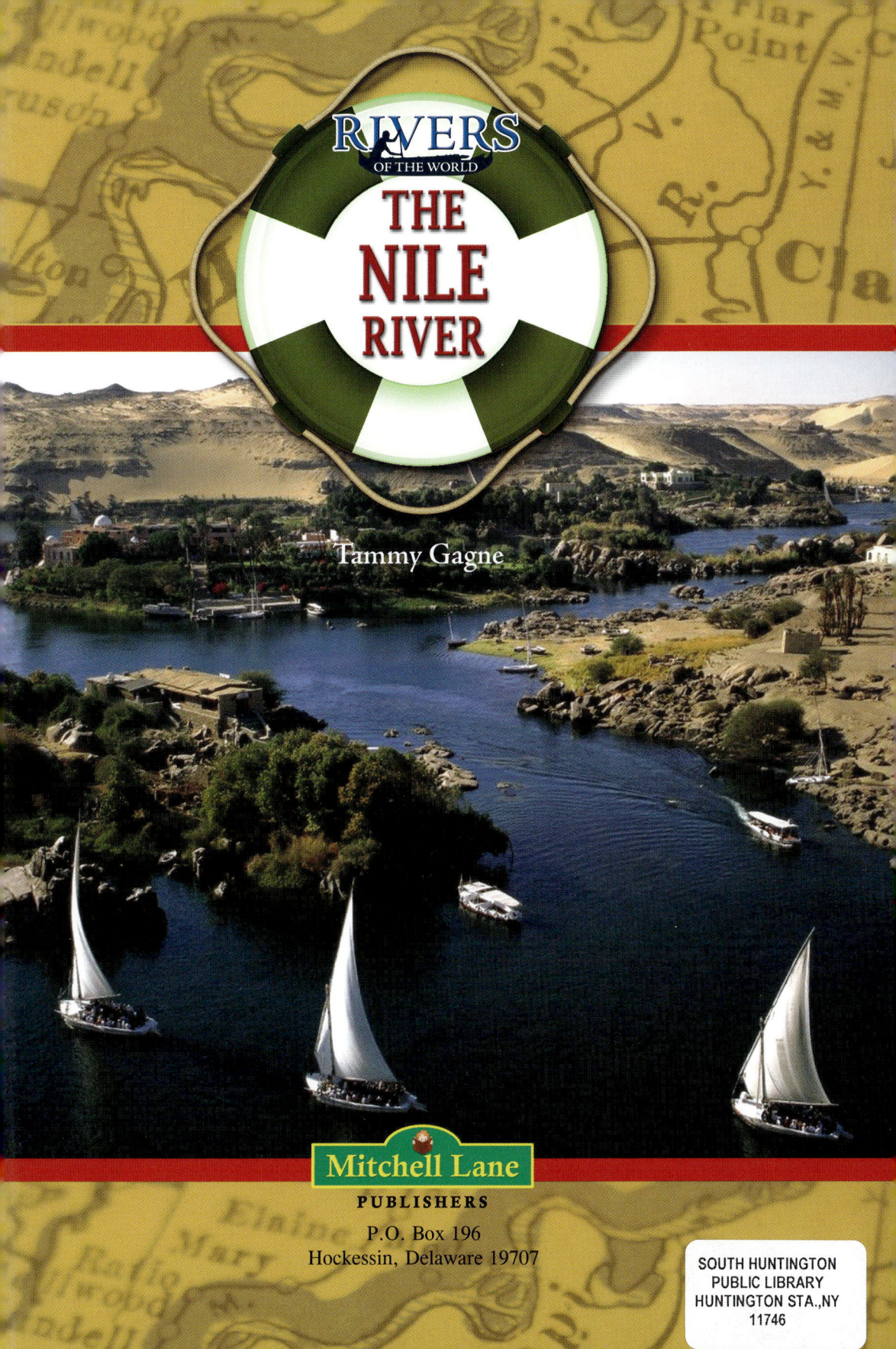

RIVERS
OF THE WORLD

The Amazon River
The Nile River
The Ganges River
The Mississippi River
The Rhine River
The Tigris (Euphrates) River
The Yangtze River
The Volga River

J 962
Gagne

Copyright © 2013 by Mitchell Lane Publishers

All rights reserved. No part of this book may be reproduced without written permission from the publisher. Printed and bound in the United States of America.

PUBLISHER'S NOTE: The facts on which the story in this book is based have been thoroughly researched. Documentation of such research can be found on page 44. While every possible effort has been made to ensure accuracy, the publisher will not assume liability for damages caused by inaccuracies in the data, and makes no warranty on the accuracy of the information contained herein.

Printing 1 2 3 4 5 6 7 8 9

Library of Congress
Cataloging-in-Publication Data
Gagne, Tammy.
 The Nile river / by Tammy Gagne.
   p. cm.—(Rivers of the world)
 Includes bibliographical references and index.
 ISBN 978-1-61228-294-7 (library bound)
 1. Nile River—Juvenile literature. I. Title.
DT115.G35 2012
962—dc23
                                         2012009467

eBook ISBN: 9781612283678

PLB

CONTENTS

Chapter One
   The Giver of Life 5
   The Story of Osiris 11

Chapter Two
   Explorers of the Nile 13
   Lady Florence Baker 19

Chapter Three
   Growing, Growing, Gone 21
   Fast Facts 25
   The Sahara Desert 29

Chapter Four
   Modern Business in an Ancient Land 31
   Blue Nile Falls 35

Chapter Five
   Looking Toward the Future 37
   Longest No Longer? 41

Chapter Notes 42
Works Consulted 44
   Books 44
   On the Internet 44
Further Reading 45
Glossary 46
Index 47

At sunset the Nile River looks serene, but this major waterway is anything but quiet. Millions of people travel along the Nile every day. The river is an important source of food, irrigation, and transportation.

CHAPTER 1

The Giver of Life

Alexander the Great, Julius Caesar, Cleopatra, Helen of Troy, King Tut, and Napoleon. What do all of these people have in common? The answer: At one time or another, each of these historical figures traveled along the Nile River. This mighty river isn't just part of the past, though. Millions of people make their way up and down the Nile every day. African farmers, fishermen, and other local people rely on it daily for their survival.

The Nile is the longest river in the world. The word "Nile" comes from the Greek word *neilos,* which means river valley.[1] Measuring 4,145 miles (6,671 kilometers) from one end to the other, the Nile begins in the country of Uganda, where it is known as the White Nile, and flows all the way to the Mediterranean Sea off the northern coast of Egypt. The Blue Nile, which joins the White Nile in Sudan, begins in Ethiopia.

People have been exploring and traveling the Nile for many centuries. Numerous explorers have

CHAPTER 1

journeyed into Africa to help map this long and winding river. Most of these voyages of exploration took place at least a century ago—in some cases thousands of the years in the past—but to this day people still set out to discover new things about this waterway. Not a single one of them, however, has made it all the way from its mouth to its source in a single trip.

The Nile and its tributaries flow through 10 different countries. The White Nile flows from Lake Victoria in Uganda through South Sudan,

The Giver of Life

Sudan, and Egypt. The White Nile is joined by the Blue Nile, which begins at Lake Tana in Ethiopia. Tributaries run through Zaire, Kenya, Tanzania, Rwanda, and Burundi.

Although the White Nile is longer, the Blue Nile carries more water. When it is at its peak, it supplies up to 85 percent of the Nile's water, whereas the White Nile provides about 15 percent. In addition to the White Nile and the Blue Nile, the Nile has two other major tributaries, the Sobat and the Atbara. All 10 countries also have smaller tributaries that flow into either the Nile or Lake Victoria.

In the highest regions, the Nile plunges over several breathtaking waterfalls. After leaving the Nalubaale Hydroelectric Power Station dam, the White Nile snakes through mountains and falls over cliffs. The water slows down a bit near Lake Kyoga, but then it drops again at Murchison Falls, where the descent is 131 feet (40 meters). The Blue Nile also has its share of waterfalls. The best known of these, Tis Isaat Falls (also known as Blue Nile Falls), is the second largest waterfall in all

Blue Nile Falls in Ethiopia

CHAPTER 1

of Africa, with a descent of 148 feet (45 meters). Its name means *smoking fire*.²

Each country the Nile passes through depends on the Nile greatly, but none so much as Egypt. On average this country receives less than an inch (20 millimeters) of rainfall each year. Because of these arid conditions, the Egyptians rely on the Nile for their most basic needs. About 97 percent of Egypt's water comes from outside the country by way of the Nile. The river begins in a much more humid region that receives close to 40 inches (1,000 mm) of rain annually.³

The Egyptian people often refer to the Nile as the "giver of life." Without this mighty river, they couldn't grow food or raise livestock. They couldn't wash their clothing and other belongings. The Nile also supplied them with many useful products, such as papyrus.

Egypt's territory encompasses about 387,000 square miles (slightly over 1,000,000 square kilometers). Of all this territory, though, only a tiny portion is inhabited. About 95 percent of the country's population lives on less than five percent of the land, mostly along the Nile.⁴ The most densely populated area is the river's delta. This region begins where the Nile splits into two much smaller branches: the Damietta and the Rosetta. The triangle of land that lies between these tributaries contains the most fertile soil of the country.

Before dams were built, the Nile would rise each year during Africa's warmest months. The flooding left dark silt all over the surrounding earth when the water returned to its normal level. The ancient Egyptians called the river *Ar* or *Aur,* which means "black," for this reason. Because the silt nourished the soil and allowed crops to flourish, the Egyptians saw this annual flooding as a gift from the gods.

The Egyptian people aren't the only beings whose lives depend on the Nile. The river and its banks are home to numerous wildlife species. Crocodiles, elephants, giraffes, and hippopotamuses are just a few of the many exotic animals that live in and around these waters. Thirty different species of snakes can be found in or along the river. Of these more than half are venomous.

The Giver of Life

More than 100 species of fish live in the Nile. While perch can be found all over the world, Nile perch are different. Some weigh more than 175 pounds (79 kilograms).[5] Smaller, yet still good-sized fish found in the river include several species of catfish, the elephant-snout fish, and the tiger fish. The smallest fish found in the river and its tributaries are the barbel and the bolti.

One of the most unusual animals that live in the swamps and ponds fed by the Nile is the lungfish. This is truly a fish out of water, at least when necessary. Unlike other fish, which only receive oxygen through their gills, the lungfish has both gills and and a lunglike organ called the swim bladder. The swim bladder enables the animal to breathe air. If its habitat dries up, the lungfish buries itself in the mud. It then grows a protective film that shields it from the sun. The lungfish can survive inside this cocoon for several months at a time. When the water returns, the film dissolves, releasing the fish.

The most unusual fish species found in the Nile is the lungfish. In addition to its gills, the lungfish has a special organ called a swim bladder that enables it to breathe air.

CHAPTER 1

Thousands of pink flamingos can be seen feasting along the Nile in Ethiopia and Uganda. In addition to the shrimp that give the birds their color, the flamingos also eat water insects from the river.

   Large flocks of pink flamingoes can be found in Ethiopia and Uganda. Feasting on water insects and shrimp, they leave the minnows and smaller perch for the colorful kingfishers and African fish-eagles. In addition to these full-time residents, millions of other birds stop in this area every year in the course of their migration southward.

   Because the Nile is so very long, it is home to a wide variety of plant life. The hottest, dampest areas of the river contain the tropical rain forests. In these areas bamboo, coffee shrubs, and rubber tree plants grow abundantly. As the moisture lessens, so does the lushness of the terrain. Trees become thinner and more spread out, forming open grasslands which are called the savanna. Some areas become swampy during the rainy season, but then dry out when the rain stops. These regions produce papyrus, water lettuce, and water hyacinth.

The Story of Osiris

Osiris

The ancient Egyptians worshipped many gods. One of the most important of these was Osiris. A god-king, he inherited the throne from his father, Geb. At this time Osiris discovered that his people were cannibals. He was very upset by this behavior. He made it his life's work to teach the people what to eat and how to grow food. For this reason, he became known as a god of the Earth and vegetation.

Osiris's brother Seth was very jealous of Osiris for both his title and his queen, Isis. Seth wanted the throne and Isis for himself, so he created a sinister plan. He murdered Osiris and threw the coffin containing his body into the Nile.

Isis brought Osiris back to life long enough to produce an heir to his throne. He did not return to this world, however. Their son, Horus, had to fight for his right to rule.

After his death, Osiris became known as the god of the underworld. The ancient Egyptians also believed Osiris was responsible for the annual flooding of the Nile and the rich soil it created. He was also associated with the rising and setting of the sun. So they created several festivals in his honor. The Egyptian people depend heavily on the fertile soil—and on the Nile itself—to this day.

The source of the Nile lies in Jinja (seen here). The town is approximately 50 miles (81 kilometers) from Uganda's capital, Kampala.

CHAPTER 2

Explorers of the Nile

The first known explorers of the Nile were the ancient Egyptians themselves. These early travelers only ventured so far up the river, though. None of them made it beyond the region that is now the city of Khartoum, the capital of Sudan.

By 30 BCE Egypt had come under the control of the Romans. About a century later, in 60 CE, the Roman emperor Nero sent out a team of soldiers to locate the Nile's source. These explorers were unsuccessful, thanks to the Sudd. This vast swamp in what is now the country of South Sudan makes up one of the largest wetland areas in the world. Its mass of tangled plants kept the Romans from reaching the river's source.[1]

The mysterious Nile continued to taunt the Romans for many years. An old Roman saying even suggested that locating its source was nearly impossible. *Facilius sit Nili caput invenire* means *it would be easier to find the source of the Nile*. Europeans used this phrase well into the 1800s.[2]

CHAPTER 2

Around the same time the Romans were traveling to Africa to solve this mystery, a Greek merchant named Diogenes went on a trip of his own. He entered from the continent's east coast and traveled into the heart of Africa. When he returned home, he spoke about two enormous lakes near a snow-covered mountain range. He believed that he had found what everyone else had been searching for—the source of the Nile.

The Greek-Roman geographer Ptolemy, who lived in Egypt in the second century CE, paid special attention to Diogenes's story. He considered it, along with accounts from other travelers to the region. He used the information when creating one of the earliest world maps. This highly detailed record was unlike any other that had come before it. It was thought to be one of the best resources of its kind throughout the next millennium. On this map Ptolemy labeled the snowy mountains

Ptolemy created one of the first world maps, which depicted the Nile River and the Rwenzori Mountains. At the time they were called the Mountains of the Moon.

Explorers of the Nile

Scottish explorer James Bruce asserted that the source of the Nile was Lake Tana in Ethiopia. More than a century later, he was proven wrong. What Bruce had actually found was the source of the Blue Nile.

the "Mountains of the Moon." Today they are known as the Rwenzori Mountains and are located in Uganda.

It wasn't until the late 1700s that European explorers set out to confirm the location of the lakes and mountains shown on Ptolemy's map. During this time a Scottish explorer named James Bruce traveled to Ethiopia. His journey proved to be difficult in more ways than one.

It was the "Era of the Princes" in Ethiopia, which meant the country had no central government. Instead, several different rulers claimed to be the rightful one in control. The Ethiopian people were in the midst of a complicated civil war at this time. No matter how hard he tried, Bruce could not avoid being diverted by the fighting.

Bruce was also struck with serious illness along his way. He came down with malaria more than once. He was sometimes sick for months at a time. Still, he wouldn't let these challenges dissuade him. In

CHAPTER 2

November of 1770, Bruce finally located Lake Tana, a massive body of water that cascaded into a magnificent waterfall which was unlike anything he had ever seen. He would later write that the lake "fell in one sheet of water, without any interval, above half an English mile in breadth, with a force and a noise that was truly terrible, and which stunned and made me, for a time, perfectly dizzy."[3]

Bruce thought this lake to be the source of the Nile. The war in Ethiopia lasted for nearly 100 years, about as long as Bruce's claim that Lake Tana was the Nile's source. It would later be revealed that what Bruce had discovered was in fact the source of the Blue Nile.

The mid-1800s brought British explorers to Africa. The Royal Geographical Society sent John Hanning Speke to the continent, along with the older and more experienced Richard Burton. These explorers also encountered their share of hardships, which included a difficult relationship between the two men. Burton's brash style was far from an ideal match for Speke's quiet and orderly ways. Both men were wounded when they were attacked by a native tribe in what is now Somalia. Speke nearly died from his injuries. To make matters worse, he felt that Burton thought he had acted cowardly in the skirmish. Burton and Speke managed to set their differences aside for the time being. In 1856 they set off together on another expedition. This one would change both of their lives forever. They were in search of the Nile's true source, but only one of them would find it.

Again, the pair advanced into Africa, this time from the coast across from Zanzibar. In February of 1858, they discovered Lake Tanganyika, the longest freshwater lake in the world. After exploring this body of water for three months, Burton was certain it was the source of the Nile. Since both men had fallen ill, however, they decided to halt their journey and head back east.

During their return trip, Burton and Speke heard talk of another immense body of water—a place the Arabs called Lake Ukerewe. Unlike Lake Tanganyika, which was long and narrow, this lake was far-reaching

Explorers of the Nile

John Hanning Speke (left) and Sir Richard Francis Burton (right) explored the Nile together despite their rocky relationship. Only one of them would find the river's true source, however.

in every direction. It was said to lie about 200 miles north of Lake Tanganyika.

Feeling much better at this point, Speke formed a small exploration party without Burton. In August he and his companions reached their destination. He renamed it Lake Victoria, in honor of England's reigning queen. After studying the lake's height above sea level, Speke was confident that this body of water, not Lake Tanganyika, was the source of the Nile. "Here at last I stood at the brink of the Nile," Speke wrote. "Most beautiful was the scene, nothing could surpass it!"[4]

When Speke reported his findings, Burton refused to admit defeat. He pointed out that Speke had offered no real evidence for his claim. The Royal Geographical Society responded by sending Speke back to Africa in 1860, but this trip also failed to provide proof. A disagreement about which man had in fact made the correct discovery would go on

CHAPTER 2

Burton and Speke at Lake Tanganyika

for the next several years. Finally, in 1864, the two men agreed to participate in a debate at the British Association to settle the issue once and for all.

A horrible tragedy kept the debate from happening. Speke was killed with his own gun while partridge hunting the day before the event was to take place. No one knows for sure what happened. Most people think the shooting was a terrible accident. Speke was said to have climbed over a wall with his gun cocked, causing it to fire accidentally. Burton believed that Speke committed suicide out of fear of facing him in the debate. He wasted no time in sharing this belief with the public.[5]

In 1869, a Welsh journalist named Henry Morton Stanley was sent to Africa by the *New York Herald* to search for yet another explorer. David Livingstone, a Scottish missionary, had set off in search of the Nile's source in 1866. He had scarcely been heard from since this time. Like so many others, Livingstone had fallen ill on his journey. When Stanley located the explorer in 1871, he uttered four simple words for which he will forever be known: "Dr. Livingstone, I presume?"[6]

After Livingstone's death in 1873, Stanley decided to return to the African continent. Two years later he confirmed that John Speke had been right. The source of the mighty Nile was indeed his Lake Victoria.

Lady Florence Baker

Lady Baker

Many men set out to explore the Nile. Some were much more successful than others. Not all the explorers of the Nile were men, however. In 1861, a couple by the name of Samuel and Florence Baker embarked on a journey to find the source of the river. Samuel was a friend of John Hanning Speke and had read about his travels to Africa.

At this point in history it was most unusual for a woman to go along on such a dangerous trip, but Florence—who was just 20 at the time—refused to stay behind. Together the pair traveled along the Nile from its mouth in Egypt. Traveling this route was no easy task, as it took them through the Sudd.

Speke had identified the source of the Nile before Samuel and Florence made it that far south. This didn't stop the two of them from continuing to explore the African continent, though. They ultimately discovered and named Murchison Falls (which is located in Uganda) and Lake Albert (which forms part of the border between Uganda and the Democratic Republic of the Congo). These accomplishments are particularly impressive considering they had a much smaller exploration party than most of the other explorers at this time.

Samuel and Florence returned to Britain in 1865, four years after they had set out in search of the Nile's source. Samuel was awarded the Royal Geographical Society's gold medal. The following year he received a knighthood. Florence was not formally recognized for her part in the discovery.

Farming is a common livelihood among the people who live along the Nile.

CHAPTER 3

Growing, Growing, Gone

People have been farming along the banks of the Nile River since about 5000 BCE. Wheat and barley were among the most common crops grown at this time. In addition to making bread from these grains, early Egyptian farmers also used them for brewing beer. Some farmers also raised cattle. As more people moved into the Nile Valley from western Asia, they brought new species of livestock with them. As a result, early Egyptian farmers also had goats, pigs, and sheep.

By 3250 BCE, Egypt consisted of two separate kingdoms. Upper Egypt, the area of the Nile Valley, was known as Ta Shemau. Its rulers lived in Hierakonpolis, near what is known today as El-Kab. Lower Egypt, the region of the Nile Delta, was called Ta Mehu. The rulers of this area lived in Buto, near today's city of Damanhur. When people look at a map, it may seem a bit strange that Lower Egypt actually refers to the northern part of the country, while Upper Egypt was in the south.

CHAPTER 3

Villages began forming in Egypt near the Nile around 3250 BCE. Most were in the Delta region because of its rich soil.

It was around this time that the first villages were forming along the Nile. Farming had begun in Lower Egypt. It was becoming a more communal activity both up and down the river. It was clear, however, that the best soil was in the Delta region.

One of the most abundant crops in the Delta was papyrus. Although this plant was edible, it was mostly used for making mats, rope, and sandals. Later it would be used as an early form of writing paper.

In 3100 BCE, the ruler of Upper Egypt conquered Lower Egypt. This man, known as Menes, became the first king of a united Egypt. The country's first capital city, Memphis, was named for him.

Today the capital of Egypt is Cairo. Located on the southern end of the Nile's Delta, Cairo is home to more than 11 million people.[1] As this number is increasing, more and more of the Delta is being consumed

Growing, Growing, Gone

by the expanding city. This area contains the only land in the country that is suitable for farming, yet it is slowly disappearing. The situation is causing many Egyptians to live in poverty.

Basic crops like corn, rice, and wheat are among the most popular food items grown in Egypt. The country also produces large amounts of fruits such as bananas, dates, and oranges. Burseem, a type of clover, is also grown in great quantities. It is sold as feed for livestock. Food isn't the only type of crop grown here, however. Some of the finest cotton in the world is grown in Egypt. Known for both its softness and strength, Egyptian cotton is exported all over the world. Many people have Egyptian cotton sheets on their beds.

Egyptian cotton is exported all over the world. Here dockworkers in Alexandria load bales of the popular material for shipment during the 1920s.

CHAPTER 3

Dams like the Nalubaale Power Station in Uganda have had a large impact on life along the Nile.

Farming along the Nile has changed a great deal since the first dams were built in the mid-1800s. Today structures like the Nalubaale Hydroelectric Power Station dam in Uganda (formerly the Owen Falls Dam) use the Nile's water to produce electricity. This river that once flowed freely is now directed into canals that channel it to water crops. A prime example, the Aswan High Dam has made it possible for Egyptian farmers to grow many types of crops year round.

Creating energy from renewable resources and bringing water to dry farmlands are worthy goals. However, dams have also created some problems. Because of the dams, the annual flooding of the Nile that once kept the Egyptian soil so rich no longer occurs. Instead, the farmers must use chemicals to fertilize their soil. These treatments work fairly well, but they are less effective than the Nile's natural silt. Chemical fertilizers are also expensive. Since so many people in Egypt are poor, the cost of farming has become a burden.

Another problem the dams cause is an increased amount of salt entering the fresh water. When large amounts of salt reach the land,

FAST FACTS

Name origin: from the Greek word neilos, which means "river valley."

Countries: Burundi, Egypt, Ethiopia, Kenya, Rwanda, South Sudan, Sudan, Tanzania, Uganda, Zaire

Major Cities: Alexandria, Aswan, Cairo, Khartoum, Luxor

Primary source (White Nile): Lake Victoria, Uganda

Secondary source (Blue Nile): Lake Tana, Ethiopia

Elevations: at mouth: 0 feet (0 meters); at highest point: 8,858 feet (2,700 meters)

Mouth: northern Egypt at Mediterranean Sea

Length: 4,145 miles (6,671 kilometers)

An aerial view of the Nile

CHAPTER 3

the soil becomes useless to farmers. Water containing too much salt is undrinkable for both people and animals.

Even with the modern dams and canals, much of the farming in Africa is still done the old-fashioned way. Most Egyptian farmers, or *fellahin*, cannot afford expensive farm equipment such as tractors to aid with planting and harvesting. Instead, they rely on animals like donkeys, mules, and water buffalo to pull their plows. The majority of farms are small. They produce just enough food for the people who live and work on the land. Some farms produce one extra crop to sell.

Many farmers also use traditional methods for irrigating their crops. The *shaduf*, for example, is still used to help water small fields in Egypt. Invented in ancient times, this simple piece of equipment consists of a long pole, a bucket on a rope, and a weight. The mounted pole moves in a seesaw motion to retrieve water from a canal. The *sakia* is another ancient irrigation device. Numerous buckets are attached to this large wheel, which is turned by animals. The *sakia* provides a steadier stream of water than the *shaduf* for irrigating larger crops. Although modern water pumps are more efficient, both *shadufs* and *sakias* are still commonly used in many rural areas along the Nile.

Fishing is another common livelihood of the Egyptians. This too has been made more difficult by the dams, though. The populations of numerous fish species have dropped since the Aswan High Dam was built. Like certain birds, many fish are migratory. The dam prevents these fish from traveling upstream to spawn as they once did. Other species are declining because they aren't getting the nutrients they need from the Nile's slower moving waters. For example, there are far fewer anchovies in the eastern Mediterranean.[2]

Because there are fewer fish, competition among fishermen has increased. This has made overfishing a serious problem. According to Uganda's fisheries ministry, the number of Nile perch in Lake Victoria dropped 81 percent in just three years.[3] Many of the fish being caught from this lake are still extremely young and small. The fishermen aren't giving the fish enough time to keep their species going. At this rate,

Many old-fashioned farming methods are still used along the Nile. *Shadufs* like this one are still used to water small crops.

CHAPTER 3

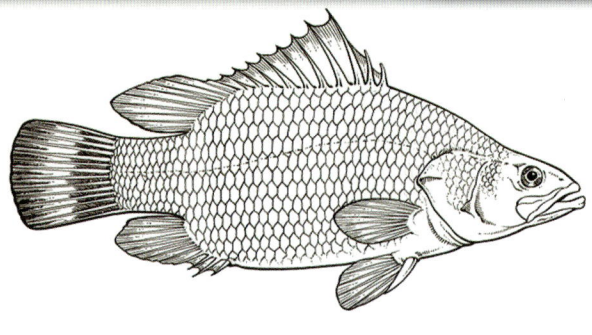

A Nile Perch

some species may end up becoming extinct.

On a more positive note, Lake Nasser—the body of water that was created by the Aswan High Dam—has been turned into a commercial fishery. Nile perch and many other species are actually thriving in its waters. It is important to note, however, that the fishing consists mostly of very small operations. The so-called commercial fishermen are mostly peasants with small wooden boats.

To the south of Egypt, life along the Nile is very different. More than twice the size of Egypt, Sudan is the largest country in Africa. It is also one of the driest with numerous deserts and arid plains. Farming in Sudan is nearly impossible unless one lives close to the Nile's waters.

Like Egypt, Sudan has a long history. The Nubians, who were named for the kingdom of Nubia, once lived in Sudan where Lake Nasser is today. Their kingdom was one of the oldest known. When the Aswan High Dam was built, however, thousands of these people lost their homes.

This was not the first tragedy the Sudanese people have endured. For centuries, Egyptians and Arabs captured the people from this area to sell as slaves. Over time many of the Arabic people who traveled to Sudan began to settle there. Many married local Sudanese. Today the majority of people in Sudan are Arabic.

Further south, most of Sudanese people living along the Nile belong to one of three main tribes: The Dinka, the Nuer, and Shilluk. For many years the people of southern Sudan were engaged in a bitter civil war. One of the reasons was religion. While the Arabic Sudanese practice the religion of Islam, the tribal Sudanese believe in spirit gods. In July of 2011, the southern Sudanese won their independence. The area where they live is now officially known as South Sudan.

The Sahara Desert

Sahara Desert

The largest desert in Africa (Antarctica is considered the world's largest desert), the Sahara Desert covers about 3,500,000 square miles (more than 9,000,000 square kilometers). Beginning in the northernmost part of the continent, the Sahara stretches from the Mediterranean Sea all the way south to the Sahel region in central Africa, where the semi-arid tropical savanna begins. East to west, the Sahara spans the land from the Atlantic Ocean to the Red Sea. The desert covers parts of numerous countries. These include Algeria, Chad, Egypt, Libya, Mali, Mauritania, Morocco, Niger, Sudan and Tunisia.

The Sahara Desert has less than ten inches of rainfall every year. The Nile is the only permanent body of water within the Sahara Desert. Most of the other water is in the form of seasonal streams or oases. The farther away from the river, the less the amount of vegetation.

In addition to being extremely dry, the Sahara is also one of the hottest places in the world. The average temperature in the region is 86 degrees Fahrenheit (30 degrees Celsius). During northern Africa's summer months, it isn't unusual for the temperature to reach 122 degrees Fahrenheit (50 degrees Celsius) or even higher. Despite this extreme heat, the Sahara becomes very cold at night.

About two and a half million people live in the Sahara Desert. Most of them travel around in a constant search for food and water.

Cairo is the capital of Egypt. It is the largest and most populous city on the entire continent.

CHAPTER 4

Modern Business in an Ancient Land

Most of the business that takes place along the Nile River today happens in Cairo. Not only is Cairo the largest city in Egypt, but it is also the most populous city in all of Africa. In addition to the millions of people who call the city home, millions more travel into Cairo every day. Most of them work there. Others attend Al-Azhar University, one of the oldest universities in the world.[1]

Walking through Cairo is an experience in opposites. If one looks up, the view is filled with tall modern buildings such as the El Gezira Tower Movenpick Hotel, the Ministry of Foreign Affairs, and the Nile City North and South Towers. On the ground, however, one will still find merchants with carts pulled by donkeys. Crowded with people and cars, the streets of Cairo are always active. With all its beauty, the city is also covered in a thick haze. Part of this can be blamed on the pollution from all the automobiles. The rest comes from the sand and dust that blow into the area from the neighboring desert.

CHAPTER 4

At one time most of the cotton grown along the Nile was sold to other countries. Egyptian cotton did in fact come from Egypt, but it was made into cloth elsewhere. Cotton remains one of the country's biggest exports today. Now, however, cloth is manufactured in Egypt as well. All sorts of other things are also made in Cairo. Food processing plants, cement and chemical factories, and steel mills are all part of the local economy.

Cairo also has an impressive film industry. Companies in the capital city produce numerous movies for Egypt and other Arabic-speaking countries. Cairo even hosts several annual film festivals. These include the Cairo International Film Festival, the Cairo International Film Festival for Children, and the Cairo Human Rights Film Festival.

Far bigger than the country's film industry is Egyptian tourism. People from all over the world have been traveling to Egypt for thousands of years. They want to see the Nile, the Pyramids of Giza, the Sphinx, and numerous other ancient monuments. Tourists also visit to see more modern attractions such as the Cairo Citadel, the Khan El Khalili Market, and the Memphis Open Air Museum.

Cairo isn't the Nile's only famous city. Alexandria, northwest of Cairo on the Mediterranean Sea, also has a long history. Named for the Greek conqueror Alexander the Great, this city was later ruled by Cleopatra, the last Egyptian queen. The Lighthouse of Alexandria once helped guide ships coming into port as long ago as 270 BCE. This structure, which stood about 380 feet (116 meters) tall, was one of the seven ancient wonders of the world. It was destroyed by several earthquakes between 956 and 1323 CE, but some of its remains have been found on the floor of the Nile.[2]

Around the same time that the lighthouse was built, Alexandria was becoming a great center for culture and learning. The Great Library of Alexandria was thought to be the largest of the ancient world. It contained more than 700,000 scrolls. These included works written by Aristotle and Plato, Buddhist texts, and the first translations of the Hebrew scriptures. Sadly, these too were destroyed over time. Not a

Modern Business in an Ancient Land

The Great Library of Alexandria no longer exists, but the Bilbilotecha Alexandrina now stands in its place.

single scroll is said to exist today, but a new library has been built in the old one's place. The Bibliotheca Alexandrina opened its doors in 2002.[3]

Like Cairo, Alexandria has also become a major player in Egyptian industry. The city is located on the Nile Delta and serves as Egypt's main port. More than 80 percent of Egypt's imports and exports pass through this harbor.[4]

Another important route for trade goods is the Suez Canal. Located just east of the Nile Delta, this manmade channel connects the Mediterranean Sea to the Red Sea. The canal makes it possible for ships to travel from one body of water to the other. Without it, vessels would have to make a much longer voyage—all the way around the southern tip of Africa—to travel between Europe and the Far East.

CHAPTER 4

Without the Suez Canal, ships like the USS *America* would have to travel all the way around the southern tip of Africa to get to the Far East.

The first canal in this area was constructed by the ancient Egyptians in 1874 BCE, but it wasn't kept up very well. It was closed and reopened many times over succeeding centuries.

Today's Suez Canal was completed in 1869, and is about 120 miles (193 kilometers) in length. When first built, the Suez Canal was about 26 feet (eight meters) deep, which meant it could allow ships weighing up to 5,000 tons to pass through it. This was the size of a typical ship in the middle of the 19th century. As ships increased in size, the canal needed to be made larger as well. This has been done several times since the canal's creation. Today the Suez Canal is about 79 feet (24 meters) deep. It can now accommodate ships weighing up to 240,000 tons.[5]

Blue Nile Falls

Blue Nile Falls

One of the most breathtaking sites along the Blue Nile is Tis Issat Falls, also known as Blue Nile Falls. Not only is this beautiful waterfall—which is located in Ethiopia—a sight to behold, but it is also extremely loud. Just imagine the sound of millions of gallons of water pouring over the cliff into a gorge below. It's no surprise that this is a popular tourist destination. One of the favorite parts for many visitors is the sight of the stunning rainbows that appear in the area regularly.

Although it is hard to believe from looking at a photo of the falls, they are virtually dry in June. This is due in large part to the nearby hydroelectric dam. By October, though, the flow of the water has largely been restored.

A Spanish filmmaker named Jordi Llompart created a striking IMAX documentary called *Mystery of the Nile* about the Blue Nile in 2005. The movie featured several scenes that were filmed at Blue Nile Falls. These scenes almost weren't part of the film, though. When Llompart circled the area from above, the falls were only a third of their size when he had last seen them. He thought for sure he wouldn't be able to get footage of them. Thankfully, the rest of the water returned a few days later. Llompart got his footage and was able to share the images with the rest of the world.

Without the Nile, life in Egypt couldn't exist as we know it today.

CHAPTER 5

Flowing Towards the Future

The Nile's future is uncertain. For centuries, much of the world has thought of Egypt as owning the Nile. It is hard to think about the country without also thinking about the river. Nearly everything that ever has happened in Egypt is linked to this water source—*the giver of life.* What would happen to the people, animals, and environment of Egypt if the Nile's waters stopped flowing into the country?

Both Egypt and Sudan do in fact have legal rights to the Nile's water. According to a treaty written in 1959, Egypt is entitled to 55.5 cubic kilometers of the river's flow, while Sudan is entitled to 18.5 cubic kilometers. These rights were granted when Britain still controlled most of east Africa.[1]

The other countries that the Nile flows through have never been pleased with this arrangement. In the past there was very little they could do about it, though. Egypt's authoritarian leaders and the

CHAPTER 5

country's strong military have kept any major changes from happening. The future may be a different story altogether.

In 2010, five countries signed their own treaty. In it Ethiopia, Kenya, Rwanda, Tanzania, and Uganda stated that each nation is entitled to a share of the river's water. The document declared that these countries no longer viewed the original treaty as lawful. Did this act grant the five countries any legal rights? This is where the uncertainty begins.

Throughout history wars have been fought over land, over religion, and even over oil. In this case, though, a war could be declared over water. Egypt has said it would view any attempt to take its water as a reason to go to war. Would the country really take this extreme action over a river? No one can say for sure. One thing is certain, though. Nearly all of Egypt's more than 81 million people depend on this river for their energy, food, and livelihoods. To put it more simply, they depend on it for their very lives.

Flowing Towards the Future

Egypt is open to making some compromises. For instance, the country would allow other countries to build hydroelectric dams of their own. The obvious condition would be that the water would have to be directed back into the river. Egypt does not want these countries using what it considers to be its water to irrigate their crops.

Are more dams the answer, though? The dams already built along the Nile are causing some serious problems. Even Egypt itself is suffering from the ill effects of the dams. Erosion is slowly decreasing the amount of land in the Nile Delta.[2]

Some people think that Egypt isn't doing enough to solve the problem. The country has offered aid to upstream countries that need more water. At the same time, Egypt is wasting an incredible amount of their own water—an estimated 21.7 billion cubic meters each year.[3] Reducing this waste would be a huge step in the right direction. Designing more efficient irrigation systems could also help.

Many people who live along the Nile make their living by fishing.

CHAPTER 5

Building a canal in the Sudd could direct more of the Nile's water to the people who need it, but doing so could hurt the animals that presently live in the Sudd.

Doing what is best for all the people along the Nile River and the environment will be tricky. Some scientists have suggested building a canal to limit water flow through the Sudd. A great amount of water is wasted in this area each year by evaporation alone. Other experts think this idea would do too much damage to the wildlife of this region.

Politics also complicate things. Today Egypt's government is in the midst of great change. In 2011, the country's long-time president Hosni Mubarak was forced out of power. The Egyptian people wanted a true democracy.[4]

No one knows how the country's new leaders will handle the problems of the Nile. Will they be able to protect Egypt's rights to the water while still allowing others fair access to it? This question may be the biggest mystery of the Nile yet.

Longest No Longer?

The Amazon

Presently, the Nile holds the title of being the longest river in the world. The Amazon in South America is the second-longest. Although the Amazon contains more water, the Nile was judged the longer of the two waterways during the 20th century. According to a team of scientists from Brazil, though, the Nile is *not* the longer river.

In 2007 these researchers went on a two-week expedition along the Amazon River. When they returned, they reported that the Amazon is 4,225 miles (6,800 kilometers) long. This new data would make the South American waterway 176 miles (283 kilometers) longer than had previously been thought.

How do the researchers explain this difference? The scientists claim that they traced the Amazon's true source to a mountain in southern Peru called Mount Mismi. Previously, the river's source was thought to lie in the northern area of the country.

If these findings are proven to be correct, the discovery would mean that the Amazon is actually 65 miles (105 kilometers) longer than the Nile. Some authorities question the accuracy of this new data. The topic will likely be debated for many years to come.

Andrew Johnston is a geographer at the Smithsonian National Air and Space Museum in Washington, D.C. After hearing about the Brazilian expedition, he pointed out that determining a river's length is extremely difficult. "Personally, I would want to know a little bit more about how they came to that number before I was comfortable saying, 'Yes this is longer.'"[5]

Chapter Notes

Chapter 1
1. Paul Barfoot, "The Nile – facts, stats and trivia about one of the world's most majestic rivers."
   http://www.bbcknowledge.com/asia/programmes/joanna-lumley-jewel-in-the-nile/nile/
2. Wild Africa—Lakes and Rivers
   http://www.bbc.co.uk/nature/programmes/tv/wildafrica/nile_blue.shtml
3. The Nile Basin
   http://www.fao.org/docrep/w4347e/w4347e0k.htm
4. National Geographic—Egypt Facts
   http://travel.nationalgeographic.com/travel/countries/egypt-facts/
5. History.com—Nile River
   http://www.history.com/topics/nile-river

Chapter 2
1. Sir John Scott Keltie, *The Partition of Africa, Part I* (Charleston, North Carolina: Nabu Press, 2010), pp. 19-20.
2. Desiderius Erasmus, *Proverbs, Chiefly Taken from the Adagia of Erasmus, with Explanations; and Further Illustrated by Corresponding Examples from the Spanish, Italian, French & English Languages, Volume 1* (Charleston, North Carolina: Nabu Press, 2010) p. 219.
3. Richard Bangs, "Stealing the Nile: Famous falls no more." msnbc.com, March 24, 2004.
   http://www.msnbc.msn.com/id/3727491/ns/us_news-environment/t/stealing-nile-famous-falls-no-more/
4. John Hanning Speke, *Journal of the Discovery of the Source of the Nile* (London: William Blackwood and Sons, 1864), p. 459.
5. Ben MacIntyre, "Upstream Costs," *The New York Times* (Book Review), December 9, 2011, p. 26.
6. BBC—History—Historic Figures: Henry Stanley (1841-1904)
   http://www.bbc.co.uk/history/historic_figures/stanley_sir_henry_morton.shtml

Chapter 3
1. National Geographic—Egypt Facts
   http://travel.nationalgeographic.com/travel/countries/egypt-facts/.
2. History.com—Nile River
   http://www.history.com/topics/nile-river.
3. Hereward Holland, "Overfishing 'annihilating' Uganda's Nile Perch." Reuters, April 16, 2009.
   http://www.reuters.com/article/2009/04/16/us-uganda-fish-idUSTRE53F3JA20090416

Chapter 4
1. Berkley Center for Religion, Peace and World Affairs: Al-Azhar University
   http://berkleycenter.georgetown.edu/resources/organizations/al-azhar-university
2. History.com: Seven Ancient Wonders of the World
   http://www.history.com/topics/seven-ancient-wonders-of-the-world/page2

Chapter Notes

3. Chad Cohen, "Egypt Opens New Library of Alexandria." National Geographic Today, October 16, 2002.
http://news.nationalgeographic.com/news/2002/10/1016_021016_alexandria.html
4. NPR: Outside Of Cairo, Egypt's Joy Is Reserved
http://www.npr.org/2011/02/12/133709027/Outside-Of-Cairo-Egypts-Joy-Is-Reserved
5. Suez Canal Authority: Canal History
http://www.suezcanal.gov.eg/sc.aspx?show=8

Chapter 5
1. Fred Pearce, "Does Egypt Own the Nile? A Battle Over Precious Water." Yale Environment 360, October 16, 2010.
http://e360.yale.edu/feature/does_egypt_own_the_nile_a_battle_over_precious_water/2297/
2. Anna Johnson, "Global warming threatens Egypt's Nile Delta." *USA Today*, August 23, 2007. http://www.usatoday.com/news/world/2007-08-23-egypt-nile-threat_N.htm
3. Egypt State Information Service: Water Resources
http://www.sis.gov.eg/en/Story.aspx?sid=177
4. "Profile: Hosni Mubarak." BBC News, May 24, 2011.
http://www.bbc.co.uk/news/world-middle-east-12301713
5. John Roach, "Amazon Longer Than Nile River, Scientists Say." National Geographic News, June 18, 2007.
http://news.nationalgeographic.com/news/2007/06/070619-amazon-river.html

The Nile River

Works Consulted

Books

Booth, Charlotte. *The Nile and Its People.* Charleston, South Carolina: The History Press, 2010.

Collins, Robert O. *The Nile.* New Haven, Connecticut: Yale University Press, 2002.

Jeal, Tim. *Explorers of the Nile: The Triumph and Tragedy of a Great Victorian Adventure.* New Haven, Connecticut: Yale University Press, 2011.

Johnston, Harry. *The Nile Quest: A Record of the Exploration of the Nile and its Basin.* Cambridge, England: Cambridge University Press, 2011.

Morkot, Robert. *The Egyptians: An Introduction.* London, England: Routledge, 2005.

Rainis, Franka. *The River Nile.* Amazon Digital Services (Kindle Edition), October, 2011.

Shipman, Pat. *To The Heart of the Nile—Lady Florence Baker and the Exploration of Central Africa.* New York: William Morrow, 2004.

Other Sources

Animal Planet
   http://animals.howstuffworks.com/fish/lungfish-info.htm

Irrigation Association—Irrigation Timeline
   http://www.irrigationmuseum.org/exhibit2.aspx

Richard Cavendish, "The Nile's Source Discovered." *History Today,* August 2008.
   http://www.historytoday.com/richard-cavendish/nile%E2%80%99s-source-discovered

Further Reading

Books
Aloian, Molly. *The Nile—River in the Sand*. New York, New York: Crabtree Publishing Company, 2010.

Banting, Erinn. *Natural Wonders: The Nile River*. New York, New York: Weigl Publishers, 2007.

Krebs, Laurie. *We're Sailing Down the Nile*. Cambridge, Massachusetts: Barefoot Books, 2008.

Pollard, Michael. *The Nile (Rivers of Life)*. London: Evans Brothers, 2010.

Wojahn, Rebecca Hogue and Donald Wojahn. *A Nile River Food Chain: A Who-Eats-What Adventure*. Minneapolis, Minnesota: Lerner Publications, 2009.

Websites
Ancient Egypt for Kids—Gifts of the Nile
   http://egypt.mrdonn.org/geography.html

National Geographic Kids—Brainteaser: Ancient Egypt
   http://kids.nationalgeographic.com/kids/games/puzzlesquizzes/brainteaseregypt/

Science Kids: Nile River Facts
   http://www.sciencekids.co.nz/sciencefacts/earth/nileriver.html

Social Studies for Kids: The Nile River
   http://www.socialstudiesforkids.com/articles/geography/nileriver.htm

Time for Kids: The Nile River
   http://www.timeforkids.com/content/nile-river

The Nile River

PHOTO CREDITS: All photos—cc-by-sa-2.0. Every effort has been made to locate all copyright holders of material used in this book. If any errors or omissions have occurred, corrections will be made in future editions of the book.

Glossary

authoritarian (uh-thawr-ih-TAIR-ee-uhn) – a governmental system in which individual freedom comes after the authority of the state.

communal (kuh-MYOON-uhl) – used or shared by everyone in a group.

debate (dih-BAYT) – a public discussion involving opposing viewpoints.

delta (DEL-tuh) – the flat, triangular area at the mouth of some rivers.

economy (ee-KOHN-uh-mee) – the management of the resources of a community.

hydroelectric (hy-droh-uh-LEK-trik) – pertaining to the production of electricity produced from falling water.

industry (IN-duh-stree) – trade, manufacturing, or general business activity.

irrigation (ir-ih-GAY-shuhn) – the artificial application of water for growing crops.

malaria (muh-LAIR-ee-uh) – a disease caused by a parasitic protozoan and transmitted by mosquitoes.

migration (my-GRAY-shuhn) – the process of moving from one region to another.

millennium (mih-LEN-ee-uhm) – a period of 1,000 years.

missionary (MISH-uh-ner-ee) – a person sent by a church into an area to educate the people, care for their health, and convert them to that church.

papyrus (puh-PY-russ) – a tall aquatic plant native to the Nile valley.

reincarnate (ree-in-KAHR-nayt) – to live again in another body.

savanna (suh-VAN-uh) – a plain containing coarse grasses and scattered trees.

silt (SILT) – earthy matter carried by moving water and left behind as a sediment.

tributary (TRIB-yuh-ter-ee) – a stream that flows to a larger river.

venomous (VEHN-uh-muss) – containing venom, or poison.

Index

Al-Azhar University   31
Alexander the Great   5, 32
Alexandria   23, 25, 32-33
Amazon River   41
Atbara River   7
birds
  African fish-eagle   10
  flamingo   10
  kingfisher   10
Blue Nile, the   5, 7, 16, 25, 35
Bruce, James   15-16
Burton, Captain Richard   16-18
Burundi   7, 25
Cleopatra   5, 32
crops
  barley   21
  cotton   23, 32
  wheat   21, 23
Damietta River   8
dams
  Aswan High Dam   24-26, 28
  Nalubaale Hydroelectric Power Station (Owen Falls Dam)   7, 24
Diogenes   14
Ethiopia   5, 7, 10, 15-16, 25, 35, 38
Egypt
  Ancient Egyptians   8, 11, 13, 34
  Cairo   22, 25, 30-33
farming   5, 21-24, 26, 28
film industry   32, 35
fish
  barbel   9
  bolti   9
  catfish   9
  elephant-snout   9
  lungfish   9
  perch   9
  tiger fish   9
fishing   9, 26
flooding   8, 11, 24
Kenya   7, 25, 38
Khartoum   13, 25
Lake Kyoga   7
Lake Nasser   28

Lake Tana   7, 16, 25
Lake Tanganyika   16-18
Lake Victoria (Lake Ukerewe)   6-7, 17-18, 25-26
Livingstone, Dr. David   18
Mediterranean Sea   5, 25-26, 29, 32-33
Menes, King   22
Mountains of the Moon (Rwenzori Mountains)   15
Mubarak, Hosni   40
Nile Delta   8, 21-22, 33, 39
Nubians   28
Osiris   11
plants
  papyrus   8, 10, 22
  water hyacinth   10
  water lettuce   10
Plato   32
Ptolemy   14
rain forest   10
Rosetta River   8
Rwanda   7, 25, 38
savanna   10, 29
Sobat River   7
South Sudan   6, 13, 25, 28
Speke, John Hanning   16-19
Stanley, Henry Morton   18
Sudan   5, 7, 13, 25, 28-29, 37
Sudd   13, 19, 40
Suez Canal   33-34
Tanzania   7, 25, 38
tourism   32
tribes   16, 28
Uganda   5-6, 10, 12, 15, 19, 24-26, 38
waterfalls
  Murchison Falls   7, 19
  Tis Isaat Falls   7
White Nile, the   5-7, 25
wildlife
  crocodile   8
  elephant   8
  giraffe   8
  hippopotamus   8
  snakes   8
Zaire   7, 25

ABOUT THE AUTHOR

Tammy Gagne is the author of numerous books for both adults and children, including *We Visit Madagascar* for Mitchell Lane Publishers. One of her favorite pastimes is visiting schools to speak to kids about the writing process. She resides in northern New England with her husband and son.

2995